W9-BFR-708

WWW.SHOREWOODLIBRARY.ORG

Louise Trapeze

Did **NOT*** Lose the Juggling Chickens

*probably

FACT: You won't want
to miss a single one!!!

#1 LOUISE TRAPEZE IS TOTALLY 100% FEARLESS

#2 LOUISE TRAPEZE DID NOT LOSE
THE JUGGLING CHICKENS

COMING SOON:

#3 LOUISE TRAPEZE CAN SO SAVE THE DAY

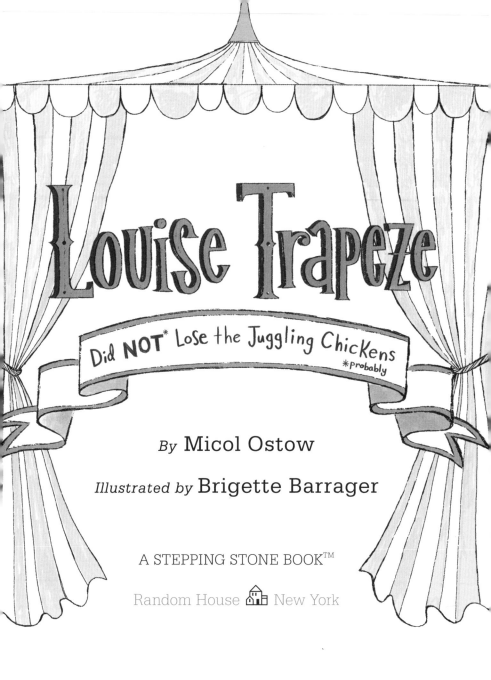

Louise Trapeze

Did NOT* Lose the Juggling Chickens
*probably

By Micol Ostow

Illustrated by Brigette Barrager

A STEPPING STONE BOOK™

Random House New York

TO SARAH M., MELISSA W., AND LYNN W.—
FOR SOAP BUBBLES AND OTHER *EUREKA!* IDEAS

Visit us on the Web! randomhousekids.com

Educators and librarians, for a variety of teaching tools,
visit us at RHTeachersLibrarians.com

Library of Congress Cataloging-in-Publication Data
Ostow, Micol.
Louise Trapeze did NOT lose the juggling chickens / Micol Ostow ; illustrated by Brigette Barrager. — First edition.
pages cm
Summary: Seven-year-old Louise, who performs in a trapeze act with her mother and father, finally gets an important job at the circus, but when things go wrong she wonders if she is really ready for new responsibilities.
ISBN 978-0-553-49743-4 (trade) — ISBN 978-0-553-49744-1 (lib. bdg.) — ISBN 978-0-553-49745-8 (ebook)
[1. Circus—Fiction. 2. Responsibility—Fiction.] I. Barrager, Brigette, illustrator. II. Title.
PZ7.O8475Lm 2016 [Fic]—dc23 2015006428

MANUFACTURED IN MALAYSIA
10 9 8 7 6 5 4 3 2 1
First Edition

✳ CONTENTS ✳

1. Baby(ish)sitting 1

2. Grown-Up Things to Do 9

3. Spaghetti Overboard! 14

4. Elephant Ears 20

5. Prettiest Please? 27

6. Real Live Proof 37

7. A Teeny-Tiny *Oh No!* 43

8. Snack Time for Chickens 54

9. Bubble Trouble 61

10. Here, Chickie Chickie! 71

11. Unsticking Ideas 78

12. Slippy Feathers 89

13. Happy-Happy-Happy 97

1

BABY(ISH)SITTING

Flip-flop-ZIP!

Petrova the Human Pretzel rolled across the floor of the Easy Trapezee tent. She had bent completely backward, grabbing her ankles so her body made a big, round wheel. Then she just started rolling away!

She rolled all the way around so she was right side up again, then let go of her ankles and—*boing!*—sprang back up to her feet like a regular, standing-up person.

"And *that's* how you do the Wheel," she said. She smiled. "It's all in the back." She did another bend to show what she meant.

"I don't know," my BFF, Stella Dee Saxophone, said. Her face was very doubtish. "Some of it looked like it was in the ankles. And the hands."

"And the front," I added.

The Wheel was Petrova's newest *contortion** for our circus performance.

* CONTORTION = a grown-up word for an extremely bendy trick!

Petrova, Stella, and I are all members of the Sweet Potato Traveling Circus Troupe. Petrova is our human pretzel. Stella and her parents have an acrobatics act that includes a real live elephant named Clementine. And *my* family is Mama, Daddy, and me, Louise Trapeze! Together, we're the Easy Trapezees! Can you *even*?

FACT: Flying on the trapeze is my most favorite of all the circus acts. Flying!!! Like a circus superhero!

Being in a traveling circus means lots of fun, ex-citing, adventure-ish times in lots of different places. This month, the Sweet Potatoes were performing in Funky Town.

(*Funky Town* is a special name that Stella and I made up. We like to be *unique*. We have lots of secret, just-for-us words and names for things.)

And tonight, Mama and Daddy were having their own fun adventures with Max Saxophone and Ms. Minnie Dee!*

*Also known as: Stella's parents

They all went out to a fancy, grown-up dinner at a restaurant in town.

That's why Petrova was babysitting us. Because even though we're both seven years old now, we're still *young enough for trouble,* as Mama likes to say.

Except I wish it weren't called *babysitting*. The word *baby* is right in there! There should be a more grown-up name for it. Maybe Stella and I can come up with one!

At least Petrova was giving us a sneak peek at her newest contortions while she watched us. That was exciting. Also, she was letting us help cook dinner, which is an *extra*-grown-up thing to do! We were making a giant pot of spaghetti on the hot plate in our tent. Stella and I took turns stirring the noodles.

FACT: Stirring the noodles is one of the very most important jobs of cooking spaghetti.

The pasta was boiling away, so I decided it was the perfect time to practice the Wheel myself. It could even help improve my form on the trapeze! *Practice makes perfect,* as Mama likes to say.

"Stand back," I said to Stella and Petrova. They each nodded and took one step away from me so I had more space.

"I'm going to try the Wheel," I said. "Here goes nothing!"

First, I "limbered up" with some stretches. That's the fancy way of saying I shook my muscles until they were warm and ready for twisting. Then I lay on my back on the ground, planted my hands next to my ears, and pushed up high-high-high until I was all curved-up backward like a bridge. Or better yet, like a rainbow! (Rainbows are the prettiest.)

"Go, Louise!" Stella cheered.

"You've got it!" Petrova called.

It wasn't totally, one hundred percent, a wheel— more like halfway there—but I was feeling very

bendy! *Hooray!* If I could only bring my hands closer to my ankles, I'd be able to grab hold of them, just like Petrova.

But then! As I inched my fingers along the ground, I felt something tickle-ish on my forehead. Something *furry.*

"Cheeze Louise!" I called. *Bump-thump-knock!* Down I went.

A face popped right in front of mine, shiny brown-ish eyes blinking away.

Shiny, brownish, *ferrety* eyes.

Linus!

2

GROWN-UP THINGS TO DO

There is one important thing to know about the Sweet Potato Circus:

FACT #1: I have gazillions of friends here. Almost everyone in our circus family is super-ultra nice and fun to be around.

But there is another, *also*-important thing to know:

Fact #2: I also have one major, big-time enemy.

And that enemy has a pet ferret.

"Ferret-breath Fernando!" I called out. I jumped up and scratched the tickle-ish part of my forehead where Linus, Fernando's ferret, had rubbed.

There he was: Fernando Worther, Ringmaster Riley's son. He thinks he's the boss of the worldwide universe because he's nine. *So what?* I almost stuck my tongue out at him, before I remembered what an unmature thing that is to do.

Linus the Ferret sat on Fernando's shoulder. He peered at me with little ferret eyeballs. Linus is not *actually* a trained circus ferret, just a pet that Fernando taught to sneak up on enemies and tickle with his furry, whiskerish snout.

"You gooberhead!" I said. (I meant Fernando. It's not Linus's fault that his person teaches him mean tickling tricks.)

"Sorry," Fernando said. He shrugged. But he didn't really look sorry at all. "Linus was just curious about what you were doing, all upside down like that."

"I was practicing the Wheel," I grumbled. "Until you interrupted. What are you even doing here?"

"My dad wanted me to drop off this schedule change for your parents," Fernando said. He held out a sheet of paper. "And he wants to meet with them to go over some things tomorrow." He gave one to Petrova. "You get one, too. All the adults do."

"Well, our parents aren't here," I said. "They went out to a fancy restaurant for dinner."

"I'll hang on to the schedules," Petrova said. She took the papers from Fernando.

"Oh, I see!" Fernando said, smirking. "So Petrova's

babysitting you two tonight, huh?" The way he said *babysitting* made it sound extra unmature.

"So what?" Stella asked.

Fernando shrugged. "My dad is out tonight, too. But he trusted me to hand out the schedules without him. And to watch Linus. And he *didn't* ask anyone to babysit me." He raised his eyebrows at me. "I must be more *responsible* than you guys."

Ooh, that made me angry. "No way!" I said in a shoutish voice.

"Face it, Louise," he said. "I'm the one here with *actual* grown-up things to do."

"Taking care of a stinky ferret is not so special," I snapped. I pointed to where the

spaghetti was bubbling on the hot plate. "Look! Stella and I are *cooking dinner*! How grown-up is *that*?"

Petrova nodded. "It's true. They're excellent helpers."

Petrova was being nice. But I didn't want to be a helper! I wanted to be *responsible,* just like Fernando!

Well, I'd show them. The pasta was boiling. So that meant it was ready. And I knew just what to do.

3

SPAGHETTI OVERBOARD!

I pointed to the spaghetti pot again. "Look," I said. "The pasta is ready. I'll just drain it so we can eat." I was sure Fernando had never made a spaghetti dinner for *his* family all by himself!

So there! I thought, running to the hot plate.

"Careful, Louise! The water is hot!" Petrova called. She rushed after me. "Don't touch!"

Steam was rising up-up-up from the bubbling pot.

Actually, it looked like Petrova was right—that pot was too hot for me! I stepped away from the bubbling water and all its steaminess. Fernando snickered while Petrova drained the pasta into a strainer by herself. She put the strainer down on a stool by the hot plate.

"Guess you're not grown-up enough for that job, either," Fernando teased.

I glared at him. "I'm still the best helper of all times."

"You are," Petrova agreed. She gave Fernando a glance of her own. Then she turned back to me. "In fact, Louise, why don't you help me pour the drained spaghetti into that bowl?" She pointed to our little folding dinner table with a large glass bowl on top.

That sounded nice. I smiled at Petrova in an agreeing-with-her way. But then I explained, "I don't need to *help* you carry the spaghetti. I can do it all by myself!"

Before Petrova could say anything, I quick-reached and picked up the strainer. I lifted it very dramatically so Fernando could completely see all my grown-up-ness.

Except.

It turned out the strainer was *heavy*.

Super heavy.

And steamy. Like *hot-steam-burny-in-my-eyes* steamy. And I was one hundred percent probably going to drop it!

"Agh!" I grunted, and clenched my fists tight-tight-tight around the strainer. But I still couldn't hold it up.

Oh no!

The strainer tilted, spilling spaghetti into a giant, slippery mountain at my feet.

"Spaghetti overboard!" Fernando called. He snickered again.

Petrova stood next to me. She looked sadly at the spaghetti mountain. "Louise," she asked, "why didn't you let me help you with that?" She didn't sound angry, just confused.

But *actually,* it wasn't confusing at all. It was very easy to understand:

I didn't *want* Petrova to have to help me. Not with my circus tricks, not with cooking spaghetti, not with anything. *I didn't want help from grown-ups.*

I wanted to be more like *Fernando.* Even if he *was* a big-time gooberhead.

Can you *even?*

4

ELEPHANT EARS

Thank goodness gracious, it was easy to clean up the spaghetti-mountain spill. Petrova and Stella were very nice about it. Petrova didn't even say anything to Mama and Daddy about it when they came home. And when we woke up in the morning from our sleepover party, Stella didn't mention it, either.

FACT: A good best friend does not remind you of your spaghetti mountain mistakes the next day.

"Do you want to work on the Wheel some more this morning?" I asked Stella after we were all dressed and ready for the day.

Stella smiled. "Yes!" she said. But then she wrinkled her forehead. "But wait. I have to give Clementine her breakfast right now."

"Oh." My mouth turned down. First Fernando and Linus, and now Stella and Clementine. *Everyone* had real, grown-up responsibility except me!

It's a good thing I am way too mature to be jealous of Stella. I worked hard to push a smile onto my face.

But Stella could tell I was feeling saddish. "Why don't you help me?" she offered.

Stella and I share some Important Circus Jobs that we do together, like brushing Stefano Wondrous's Wonder Dogs' coats. But I wanted a job that was just mine-mine-mine.

Helping was totally the opposite of *mine-mine-mine*. But it was better than nothing. Also, it was nice that Stella wanted to make me feel better. "Okay!" I said.

Clementine was waiting for us when we got to her pen. She waved her trunk in a good-morningish way. Stella unlocked the gate and in we went.

"I'll go fill her food trough," Stella said. She went to the shed at the back of the pen that stored the bazillion kinds of plants that elephants like to eat.

Fact: Clementine loves eating plants—
ALL plants! One time she even
ate an ENTIRE Christmas tree,
branches and all!!!!

While Stella was in the shed, I thought about what to do to be helpful. It wasn't long before a *eureka!* thought popped into my brain.

There was a tub of water off to one side of the pen. A spray bottle and a towel were next to it, sitting on top of a small stepladder.

"I'll get your morning sponge bath started!" I told Clem. She nodded to say this was an excellent plan.

I pulled the bottle, the towel, and the ladder closer to Clementine and climbed up-up-up until I was just at the height of her ear. "Let's scrub those ears out before they sprout potatoes!"* I told her.

*That's what Mama says when I'm in the bath with extra-dirty ears. Except I never saw an actual human person with potatoes growing out of their head.

Clementine opened her eyes wide. "There, there," I said. I patted her very gently. Then I spritzed away at her giant elephant ear.

Splish-splash-splosh! Clementine shook her head like craziness. She trumpeted loudly. *Yikes!* What was happening?

Stella came running from the shed. "Oh no!" she cried. "Louise, you have to be careful not to spray the inside of Clem's ears! She *hates* the way that feels!"

Uh-oh! I didn't mean to hurt Clementine!

I rushed down from the stepladder. "I'm sorry!" I said to Stella. "I didn't know about elephant ears!"

"It's okay," Stella said. "We know it wasn't on purpose." She climbed up the ladder and patted Clem's ear off with my towel.

When she was done, she looked at me. "But why didn't you just wait for me to come out of the shed? Then I could have helped you do it right."

My face got very hottish and my throat felt lumpy.

I swallowed and tried to push the lumpiness down. "I'm sorry," I said again.

I *was* sorry. But I was also wondering two things:

1. Why did everyone think I needed help all the time?

2. And even worse . . . why did it seem like they were *right*?

5

PRETTIEST PLEASE?

Flip-swoosh-flop! Mama whooshed over her trapeze bar, graceful as a gazelle.*

*GAZELLE = a very graceful, fancy animal that is sort of like a deer (if a deer was a prima ballerina in satiny toe shoes)

After I left Stella and Clementine, I went to find Mama and Daddy. Their giant, grown-up-sized trapeze rig is always set up behind our tent.

Mama swung out and prepared for a trick. She hooked her legs under the bar and hung by her knees. Then she let go, arched back, and *reach-reach-reached* for Daddy's hands. He caught her, and they swung— *whiiizzz!*—back to Daddy's side of the trapeze. As

their swinging slowed down, Daddy held his arms out
and Mama dropped to the net below the trapeze bars.

Boing-flip! Mama's face popped up from the net.
"Lou!" she called, smiling at me. "How was Clem's
breakfast?" She blew her shiny bangs off her forehead
and slid to the edge of the net. She rolled off so she
was next to me on the grass again.

I shrugged. "Okay," I said.

"Hmm," Mama replied. "Then why do you look so down?"

I sighed. "It's just that . . . I also tried to give her a bath. But I forgot Clem doesn't like when water gets sprayed inside her ear," I said. "So that was a mistake I made."

"Ah," Mama said. "Is Clem okay?"

"Yes," I said.

Mama nodded. "Well then, it was just one mistake. Everyone makes mistakes, Lou."

Except it *wasn't* just one mistake. There was also the spaghetti-slipping mistake from last night. But I for sure wasn't going to bring *that* up!

"Everyone else in the circus has grown-up things to do except me," I said. "Petrova babysits. *And* she can do the Wheel. Stella takes care of Clementine. Fernando watches Linus. And he helps his dad deliver important messages!"

I gave Mama my saddest eyes of ever. "I don't have any actual, grown-up responsibilities that are only-my-own."

"What about your Important Circus Jobs?" Mama reminded me.

"Like brushing the Wonder Dogs! And oiling Clara Bear's unicycle," Daddy added. He'd climbed down from the trapeze platform while I was talking to Mama. He sat down with us and made a listening face.

How could I make them understand? "But I have to *share* my Important Circus Jobs with Stella. So they're not only-my-own."

"Are you *really* ready for your own responsibilities?" Mama asked.

"Yes! And I'm seven now!" I said. "I'm extremely mature! I'm totally, one hundred percent, ready for responsibility that is *just mine.*"

And I *was* ready. Even if I'd spilled the spaghetti. And even if I'd gotten Clementine's ear all wet. Those were both just *flukes.**

*Fluke = a crazyish mistake that will never, ever happen again

Daddy pushed one eyebrow up. "Louise," he said, "are you forgetting what happened when Miss Kitty Fantastico asked you to keep an eye on her ant farm?"

"That wasn't my fault!" I pouted. "She should have warned me to make sure the cover part was all-the-way screwed on."

(Miss Kitty Fantastico is the assistant to

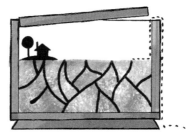

Magnificent Blue the magician. Really, she should have just used magic to keep those ants in their glass case, if you ask me.)

"And what about when you tied Tolstoy the Clown's balloon animals too loosely, and they all flew away just before show-time?" Mama added.

I made a frowny face. "It was the *wind* that took the balloons away."

(Boy, did it ever! Tolstoy had to work like craziness to get new balloon animals ready in time for our show. That was *terrible*.)

"And then there was—" Mama started.

I cut her off. I couldn't help myself. "Never mind!" I said. My voice was loud and my face was tamale hot.

I took a deep breath and tried to be more calm.

"Those things all happened when I was *still six*," I explained. My voice was more regular-person now. "I've grown a lot since my seventh birthday. I'm *extra*-super mature now. I promise."

Mama and Daddy looked doubtish. But they were still listening.

"*Please* can I have a mature responsibility of only-my-own?" I didn't care what, as long as it was *something* grown-up. "Prettiest please with purple ponies* on top?"

★Purple ponies are the most unique kind of ponies, because I made them up myself, inside my brain.

Daddy looked at Mama. "We're not saying *no*, Lou—" he said.

"HOORAY!" I exploded into a little happiness dance.

"*But* we're not saying yes yet, either," Mama finished. "We'll think about it."

"Hmm." A lot of the time, *We'll think about it* is a grown-up way of saying *We're probably going to say no later.* But they weren't saying no now!

"In the meantime," she said, "maybe you can think about ways to show us that you're more mature and responsible now."

"I will!" I said. I nodded my head a bunch.

I just hoped those imaginary purple ponies in my brain had some ideas. Because I didn't have any of my own yet.

6

REAL LIVE PROOF

After-lunchtime on the Sweet Potato grounds is a very quiet, resting-and-being-still time. Ring-master Riley calls it siesta hour, which is a fancy, Spanish way of saying *nappish time*. Most of the Sweet Potatoes were tucked away in their tents, sleeping or reading or finding other ways to not be noisy.

Mama and Daddy were in bed, snoozing away. Morning practice had tired them out. I tried lying

down on my bed to rest like them. But my eyelids would *not* stay shut!

I was not at all nappish. My brain was running in thinking circles inside my head!

Mama and Daddy wanted *actual*, real live proof that I was a very responsible seven-year-old. So that's what I had to give them! How hard could real live proof be to get?

Blink-blink-blink went my eyelids.

Think-think-think went my brain.

It felt like foreverness before I had a good idea of how to show how grown-up I was.

But then:

I had the most perfect idea in the whole worldwide!

FACT: Oiling Clara Bear's unicycle so it doesn't squeak is one of Stella's and my Important Circus Jobs.

On a lot of days, we take care of that first thing in the morning. But we hadn't yet today.

So I decided: I'd oil Clara's unicycle *myself*!

And if a-little-bit-oiled was good for Clara's unicycle, then a-*lot*-bit-oiled would be *even better*!

Daddy is always talking about the importance of *trying our best*. And I could for sure try harder to oil the unicycle the very best!

It was probably the most *mature* idea I'd ever had.

We keep the oil can in the supply trailer, right next to the box office tent (where the tickets are sold). When I got to the trailer, no one was around. That was perfect.

The door to the trailer was unlocked. *That* was even perfect-*er*. I went into the trailer and took the can off its shelf. I brought it over to the equipment trailer next door, where Clara's unicycle was leaning—perfectly—

up against a corner, right next to Koko Rico the Monkey's monkey-sized ukulele.

FAct: Monkeys are excellent ukulele players.

I took the unicycle out onto the grass in front of the trailer and poured oil all over the spokes of the wheel. Then I rubbed that oil in extra well with a special towel. Soon the unicycle was moonbeam shiny.

When I was done, the can was almost empty. The towel was greasy and black, and the unicycle wheel was as slippery as the banana peels Tolstoy uses in his act. When I turned it, it spun faster than Mama doing flips on her aerial hoop!

Perfect-est! I thought. This was the best-oiled unicycle wheel of all times. I couldn't wait for Clara to give it a try!

A TEENY-TINY *OH NO!*

After I finished oiling Clara's unicycle, I waited outside of her pen for her to wake up. It felt like siesta would never be over. Inside my body, butterflies of excitement were exploding all over! I wanted to grab Koko Rico's ukulele and run circles around Clara's pen playing music, just so she'd wake up. Then I could show her my big surprise.

Finally, the little hand on the box office clock said 2:00. Tent flaps and trailer doors peeled open. Sweet

Potatoes poked their heads outside, blinking in still-sleepyish ways. I waited as patiently as I could for Clara Bear, even though my excitement butterflies were ready to fly to the moon.

Fact: Excitement butterflies have LoTS of energy.

At last, Clara Bear snuffled, turned over, and stood up. She lumbered over to me. She was blinking and rubbing her eyes, too. Clara *loves-loves-loves* siesta time. It's her favorite part of the day, besides snack time. (Bears are excellent nappers.)

"Guess what!" I said to Clara with my most excited face on. "I have a *huge* surprise for you." I wheeled her unicycle over.

"I oiled it *extra*!" I explained. "Let's see how fast you can go now!"

Clara nodded. I led her to the top of the nearest circus ramp, which was set up just behind the box office. It was

very quiet there. "I guess people are still siesta-ing," I said to Clara. "But we can practice anyway!"

Carefully, Clara climbed onto her unicycle. Once she was up, she pedaled her hind legs. They went slowly at first. But that wheel still spun shiny and quick.

Then Clara's legs started moving faster and faster. Her unicycle wheel spun *whizz-swish-zip.* Now that it was double-oiled, that unicycle was the fastest thing

I'd ever seen . . . *way* faster than Mama on her aerial hoop.

Actually, maybe that unicycle was a little *too* fast now?

Clara's eyes were wide. Her snout was turning in a scaredish way. Her legs were pedaling so quickly she was bouncing in her seat! And—*oh no!*—her unicycle wheel was wobbling left and right!

Zip-whizz-swish! The unicycle pitched over to one side. Then it *kaboom*ed over the edge of the circus ramp!

"Clara!" I shouted. She was still zig-zag-*zoom*ing along. Her legs were swishing away. Her eyes were the widest ever.

Uh-oh! Clara was rolling right toward a tree! "Watch out!" I called.

At the exact lastest minute, Clara turned on her

unicycle to the right. *Screech!* She *swoop*ed to one side and missed the tree by the tiniest smidge!

"Clara!" I ran to her and untangled her from the unicycle. I checked her carefully for any scrapes and bruises. Clara snuggled tight-tight-tight up against me.

I felt terrible. "Are you okay?"

Clara nodded.

"Thank goodness gracious," I said. I sighed my most relieved-person sigh.

Then I felt a shadow over my shoulder. When I turned around, Mama was standing behind me. She made questioning eyebrows at me.

"What's going on here, Louise?" she asked.

I swallowed. "We . . ."

I put a hand on Clara's fuzzy, bearish shoulder. "We were just practicing a new trick with the unicycle. *Practice makes perfect.* Right, Clara?" I gave her

a Very Important Look. As long as Clara was okay, maybe Mama didn't need to know I'd made another mistake.

Clara gave a tiny nod to show she understood. She looked straight at Mama in a very agreeing way.

Mama looked thoughtful. "Are you *sure* you don't need any help, Louise?" she asked finally.

"Totally sure," I said in my most serious-business voice. I was so tired of help from grown-ups!

"Okay," Mama said. "Because I have to meet with Ringmaster Riley right now, so I don't have time for drama."*

*DRAMA= a Mama word for making a big. huge.stinky deal about something. (Usually something small and silly.)

"No drama here!" I chirped.

Mama sighed, but she didn't ask any more questions. "Great," she said. "I'll be back as soon as I can."

The minute Mama walked off, I checked Clara Bear from top to tail to be one hundred percent sure she was a-okay. She was. What a relief!

She waved a paw at me to tell me she needed to get back to practicing with her trainer, Mary Lou-Lew. And then she gave a bearish wink to show she wouldn't ever tell about how I oiled her wheel too much.

Once Mary Lou-Lew led Clara away, I let out another giant sigh. So much sighing! This day was not turning out the way I planned!

The bad news was, I still hadn't proved to anyone how responsible I could be.

The *worse* news was, I had no idea how to do that!

But before I could think about it any more, Chuck Cluck came running up. He was breathing hard, and his face was red.

"Louise!" he said. "Thank goodness you're here! Your parents and the others are meeting with Ringmaster Riley now. And I have an *emergency*!"

My ears perked up. An *emergency* probably needed a mature, grown-up person to fix it. And Chuck Cluck came to *me*!

"What is it?" I asked.

"I have to run to town to get the chickens' skate-boards repaired before tomorrow night's show. And the shop closes in an hour. There's no time to waste!"

Was he saying what I thought he was saying?

"I need someone to watch over the chickens while I'm out," Chuck said. "I know you've never watched them on your own before, but there's no one else. And I'll be back before you know it."

"Cheeze Louise and holy trapeze!" I shouted. "I'll take *perfect* care of the chickens, I promise! Triple purple pony swear!"

Chuck smiled. "Thanks, Louise," he said. "You're a lifesaver. And I'll rush right back. You won't be alone for too long."

I *loved* being called a *lifesaver*. I threw my arms around Chuck. "Don't worry! You don't even have to rush! I am totally and completely, one hundred percent, ready for this!"

Chuck Cluck quickly showed me how to open and shut the latch to the chicken coop. He told me where he keeps the chicken feed and explained all about what to give the chickens for snack time.

(He feeds them a special seed-shaped cereal that he says is delicious to chickens. But for regular human people it looks like *ick!*)

"Thanks again, Louise," he said in his most serious-business voice. Then he rushed off to Funky Town with three chicken-sized skateboards tucked under his arms.

And then it was just me and the three juggling chickens: Oona, Loona, and Maude.

FacT: Oona and Loona are identical twins. Maude is their little sister.

Oona Loona Maude

"Hello, chickens!" I said in my very cheeriest voice. "I'm going to be your babysitter." (Even though they were chickens, not babies, watching them was a kind of babysitting.)

They all clucked and waved their wings in a feather-ish way. Oona waved the loudest—she is the older twin and the bossiest of the chickens. I could tell they were *very, extremely excited* to have such a mature person watching them.

"Would you like your snack now?" I asked.

They bobbed their heads, very chickeny, to say yes. I took the bag of feed that Chuck left and poured some into their bowls:

one, two, three!

They gobbled their food right  down. (I guess it really *is* delicious to them!) Then they chicken-walked to the front of their coop, Oona leading the way.

Oona clucked, and Loona flapped her wings. Maude bobbed her head down again in her shy baby-sister way. They poked their little beaks through the holes in the mesh and stared at me with chickenish eyes.

They stared and stared. I never saw chickens stare so much.

Those chickens sure looked like they wanted something. But what?

I looked at their bowls, which were completely empty. "Are you still hungry?" I asked.

They cluck-cluck-clucked! Even shy Maude was flapping her wings. They totally were!

Hmm. Chuck Cluck didn't say anything about how *much* feed to give them. And they were definitely still hungry.

"Okay," I said. "I can give you a little bit more."

Now they *all* flapped their wings like this was the best news they'd ever heard in their entire chicken lives.

I took the bag of feed into their coop again and kneeled down to pour some more into each bowl.

But then—*oops!* I dropped the whole bag on the ground!

The chickens clucked like mad. They flapped all around me and *peck-peck-peck*ed at the ground. Before I could pick the bag up again, all the feed had been gobbled up!

Yikes! It really was a lot of feed they ate. I hoped Chuck wouldn't mind.

Oona chicken-walked up to me. She flapped a wing

against my arm and gave a little chicken hiccup. That was when I noticed she had flecks of feed sticking all over her feathers.

Oh no! Loona and Maude were covered in feed, too. All three of them were filthy! Chuck Cluck would *not* be happy about that.

What was I going to do?

I thought very, very hard. I even crinkled up my forehead to help the thinking go faster.

Finally! There it was: a *eureka!* idea!

Problem: The chickens were dirty. Chuck Cluck would *not* be happy about that.

Solution: I, Louise Trapeze, would *give them a bath*! Then they would be squeaky clean again!

An eensy part of my brain was remembering how I messed up trying to give Clementine her sponge bath. But a bigger, more *mature* part of my brain said I'd learned my lesson and would be much more careful when bathing the chickens.

It was time to clean some chickens!

BUBBLE TROUBLE

In our circus, we have a fenced-in place near the Big Top tent where we keep a bunch of metal tubs for bathing the smaller animals. It's called the *bathing pen*. The bathing pen has teensy, wonder-dog-sized tubs and medium-sized tubs for animals like Clara Bear and Leo Torpedo the lion, too.

So I knew it would be easy to find a tub for three sister chickens.

"Follow me," I told the chickens. Oona looked at her sisters and bobbed her head to show that they should listen to me. I unlatched the door to their coop, and off we went.

The chickens marched straight-straight-straight in a line, Oona leading the way. She kept one wing up like she was pointing the whole entire time. Loona walked with her chicken rump wobbling side to side. Little Maude walked more slowly than her sisters, but she could still keep up. Along we marched!

All the Sweet Potatoes were out of Ringmaster Riley's meeting and busy with afternoon practice.

Tolstoy was teaching Leo how to back-flip over and through his fire hoop! (The hoop wasn't fiery now, since they were just practicing.)

Stefano Wondrous's Wonder Dogs were tap-dancing on top of upside-down buckets.

And Maharaja Moe was practicing a new tune on his recorder while his cobra, Khan, *swish-swoosh-swish*ed a little snakey dance.

Everyone was so busy practicing that they didn't notice me—or the chickens—at all. That was good. I wanted it to be a one hundred percent surprise when Chuck Cluck came back from town to find his chickens squeaky-clean.

Right away, I found exactly the right-sized tub for the chickens. It was mediumish, so all three of them could fit in it together.

"Here you go!" I popped Oona inside. She clucked and flapped with excitement. One by one, Loona and Maude jumped in after her.

FACT: Chickens love bath time!

I found the long spraying hose and turned on the water. It felt a little cold to me, but the chickens didn't mind. (They have all those feathers to keep them warm.)

I had the water, I had the bathtub, and I had the chickens. But I was still missing one thing:

The soap!

I forgot the soap!

"Don't move," I told the chickens. "Oona, you're in charge!" She gave a loud *squawk* at her sisters. They all bobbed their heads to say they would behave. "I'll be *right back.*"

I ran to the supply trailer lickety-split. It was dark and dusty inside. It took a minute for me to find the shelf of soap. At first all I could see were:

1. a box of screws for tightening tightwires and other circus equipment

2. glitter shakers for glittering-up Dinah-Mite White's cannon

3. a bin of silk scarves that Tolstoy sometimes pulls from his sleeve

But then—there they were! Bottles

and bottles of soapiness, right in the corner, on a low, Louise-height shelf.

I ran to the bottles and looked hard at all the labels. None of them said *special, just-for-chickens soap,* so I just grabbed the bottle that looked the most like bubble bath.

When I got back to the chickens, the water was way-high-up in the tub.

"Look what I have!" I said.

I opened the bottle of soap and turned it upside down over the tub. Squishy, bubbly soap ran out in a thick stream. It smelled like bubble gum.

Bubble-gum soap! That was probably the best kind of soap ever!

The chickens squawked as the bubbles bubbled higher and higher. It was almost spilling out! So I took the sprayer out of the water and laid it on the grass. The smell of bubble gum was almost making me dizzy!

Oona pecked her beak into the water quick-quick-quick. When she took it out, she clucked.

And then!

The funniest thing of the whole-entire-*evertimes* happened:

Oona *blew a bubble*!

"Wow!" I said. "That's *amazing*!"

A chicken blowing bubbles! Can you *even*?

Loona and Maude agreed. Soon they were pecking the soapy water and blowing bubbles, too. Oona's bubbles were the biggest, but Loona's were the funniest shapes. And Maude blew the most bubbles at one time. It was *so-so-so* funny!

Actually, I was laughing so hard at the chickens blowing bubbles that I didn't notice one *extremely* important thing:

The bubbles in the water were rising *high-higher-highest. Very* quickly!

The bubble bath had gone completely loony-crazy.

"Yikes!" I cried.

The bathwater sloshed over the side of the bin. Soap bubbles frothed up like a giant, foamy mountain. The chickens began clucking from scaredness. Maude's eyes were *very* wide. All three chickens were completely covered in bubbles.

And then!

There was a terrible *oh no!* moment:

Oona *jumped out of the tub and bobbled off*!

For a chicken, she was really very fast at running.

"No!" I tried to go after her. But the ground was all muddy from the hose sprayer. I slipped!

"Wait!" I called. I reached out a muddy arm.

But it was no use. Loona and Maude were off, following Oona!

(Oona really *is* the boss of the three sisters.)

By the time I pulled myself out of the mud, the juggling chickens were *G-O-N-E—gone!*

✳ **10** ✳

HERE, CHICKIE CHICKIE!

I had to figure out where the juggling chickens went!
I called to them, but there was no answer.

They were such fast runners! Maybe they'd run all
the way to Timbuktu!*

✳ TIMBUKTU = An extremely faraway country

That was when I saw it.

There was a trail of bubbly foam leading out of the bathing pen, off into the grass beyond the Big Top tent.

I was messy and sticky from bubbles and mud, but that didn't matter. I was responsible for those chickens! I had to find them and get them back to their coop right away.

I followed the bubble trail around the back of the big tent and past extra boxes of juggling pins, swords for swallowing, and an old red-and-white kettle corn cart that Ethel Teitelbaum says is *definitely* not forever broken. The bubbles got smaller and more watery the farther I went. It was harder and harder to spot the soapy patches in the grass.

Then the bubbles stopped completely.

And a squeaking sound started.

Oh no! It was Tolstoy the Clown's giant squeaky

shoes! He must have been coming from Ringmaster
Riley's meeting.

What if he guessed what I was doing? What if he
figured out that I *lost the juggling chickens*? That
would be the worst.

"Hey, Louise," Tolstoy said, smiling. His smile
seemed extra big because he was wearing his bright
red clown-makeup lips. "What are you up to out here?"

I had to quick-think of something to say. "I am . . . practicing some of the contortions Petrova taught me!" I said.

(It was a *brilliant* answer, if you ask me.)

I continued, "I came over here for some *privacy*."*

*PRIVACY= alone space for thinking or doing things that are just for you. Like how Fernando is only supposed to pick his nose in privacy, but sometimes he forgets.

"I understand," Tolstoy replied. "I like to practice new routines in private, too. I'll leave you to it!"

Phew, I thought as he walked off. That was close!

Thank goodness gracious he didn't guess my secret problem.

But then I remembered: I still *had* a secret problem! And I needed to solve it.

There were no more bubbles in the grass. I'd hit a dead end. Was this it? Was I never, ever going to track down those chickens?

No way, Jose, I thought. I looked up. I was standing right in front of two sets of metal bleachers, stacked together like a puzzle for storage.

That was when I heard it—a smallish clucking sound. That cluck sounded just like Maude!*

*Oona, Loona, and Maude each have very unique clucks. Just like how human people have unique voices!

"Maude?" I called. "Is that you? Oona? Loona?"

The clucks got a little bit louder. They sounded like they were coming from . . .

. . . under the bleachers?

I kneeled down in the grass. I bent over and flattened my head against the ground. It was hard to see under the bleachers, even in the bright-and-shiny sun.

Cluuuck!

"Eek!" All of a sudden, there was an Oona-sized beak *close-close-close* to my face. It peeked out from the dimness.

"Oona!" I could barely see her in the darkness. But there was a for-sure scared look in her little chicken eyes. "What are you doing under there?"

I heard the rustly sound of a wing flapping. "Are you stuck?" I asked.

Maude clucked sadly in a *yes* way.

"Are Maude and Loona back there with you?"

I heard two more *yes*-ish clucks from behind Oona.

"Don't worry!" I told them in my most calm, grown-up voice. "I'll get you guys unstuck."

And I would. I *had* to!

But how?

11

UNSTICKING IDEAS

FACT: The juggling chickens were stuck under the bleachers.

FACT: I, Louise Trapeze, was responsible for the chickens.

FACT: It was one hundred percent my job to get them unstuck, out of there, and a-okay!

Those were three things I knew.

But also, there was a fourth fact inside my brain. And that was:

I TOTALLY AND COMPLETELY have no idea how to unstick a chicken from under a bleacher!

I needed to do some crinkly forehead thinking to fix this problem.

I scrunched up my face tight-tight-tight. I took very deep breaths. I even closed my eyes so I could really concentrate.

But it didn't help. Not even a smidge. My brain was empty like the inside of one of Tolstoy's super-gigantic helium balloons.

Then I remembered:

Last night, when I was

trying to cook spaghetti, I didn't ask for help. And the spaghetti spilled.

And this morning, when I was giving Clem a bath, I didn't wait for help. And I got water in her ear!

I wanted to be a mature, grown-up person who didn't *need* to ask for help, ever.

But maybe . . . *just maybe* . . . asking for help is sometimes *the most grown-up thing you can do.*

It was definitely a theory.*

*THEORY: a mini-thought that still needs to be figured out all the way

Fact: *I* couldn't make my arms bendy enough to get to the stuck chickens. But there was someone else in our circus who maybe could!

Lickety-split, I ran to Petrova the Human Pretzel's

tent. But when I got there, she was nowhere to be found! "Petrova?" I called. "Are you here?"

There was a small white steamer trunk right in front of her tent. It was smaller than the tank for our dancing sea horses.*

*Lady Edwina sews tiny, sea-horse-sized bathing suits for our sea horses to wear in our show.

Slowly, the lid to the trunk opened. A long, skinny, Petrova-shaped back rose up. And then! Petrova popped her head upright, unfolded her arms, and stepped right out of that eensy-weensy box!

"Sorry," she said. She wiggled her arms and shook her head so her short, straight hair tickled her cheeks. "I was practicing a new contortion."

"Wow!" I said. That was some trick!

Then I remembered why I was looking for her in the first place. "Except, if you have a minute"—I took a deep breath—"I need your help."

"Of course. What's wrong, Lou?" she asked.

"Follow me," I said.

I took her back to the bleachers. She bent down on the ground the same way I had. She called out to the chickens the same way I had, too. They clucked sadly at her—just the way they'd clucked at me.

Petrova made herself long and slitherish like a snake. She went flat down and wiggled so the whole top of her body disappeared under the bleachers. But after a minute, she slid back out again. She was completely chickenless.

"Sorry, Louise," she said. "*I* can get in and out of there, but the chickens aren't flexible* like I am."

*Flexible = the fancy way of saying twisty like a human pretzel

My shoulders slumped. "Oh well," I said. "Thanks for trying."

Now what? The chickens were still stuck. I was totally out of *eureka!* ideas. And I needed to get the chickens free before Chuck Cluck came back from town.

And before Mama and Daddy discovered my un-responsibleness.

"Lou! I was looking all over for you." It was Stella. She was still in her practice leotard. Clementine the Elephant followed right behind her. (Clementine

always follows right behind Stella. They are like *two peas in a pod,* as Mama says.)

"I saw Chuck Cluck when he was leaving for town. He said you're watching the chickens. That is *so* mature," she said.

Stella knows exactly how important being mature is. That is one of our friendship things.

"But when I went to the chicken coop to find you, it was empty." Stella looked at me closer now. "Why are you so muddy? Where are the chickens, Lou?"

Clementine lowered her trunk to the bottom of the bleachers. She sniffed. Then she trumpeted softly.

I nodded. "They're stuck under there."

Stella gasped. "How did that happen?"

"I was giving them a bath," I explained. "But the bubble-gum soap went crazy. And when I was trying to stop the bubbles from foaming all over, the chickens flew the coop! I mean, the tub."

"I tried to get under there to help them out," Petrova said. "But it didn't work. We need to go get Ringmaster Riley. Or your parents, Lou."

"No!" I shouted. That was the worst idea in the universe. "If we tell my parents what happened, they'll *never* think I'm grown-up enough!"

"It was a mistake, Louise. Even mature grown-ups make mistakes," Petrova said. "I'm sure your parents know that."

I shook my head. "You don't understand. This is my third mistake today! First there was Clementine's ear. Then I overoiled Clara Bear's unicycle. She went sliding all over."

"Uh-oh," Stella said, her eyes wide.

"*Uh-oh* is right! That wheel was so-so-so slippery . . . ," I started.

But then I stopped.

Because when I said *slippery,* an imaginary light-bulb popped up over my head.

There it was: my *eureka!* idea!

I knew *exactly* how to rescue the chickens.

"You're a genius!" I told her, giving her a great big hug.

"I am?" Stella asked. "Hooray for me!" She waved her arms like she was excited. "But what now?"

"Just wait," I told her. "We are totally and completely going to fix this!"

12

SLIPPY FEATHERS

Stella and I ran to the supply trailer, fast-fast-fast. The oil for Clara's unicycle was just where I'd left it. *Perfectamundo!** This was definitely going to work!

*Perfectamundo = a special, Louise-fancy way of saying super-amazing!

I grabbed the oil can. Stella grabbed one of her own for good measure.

"Let's go!" I said. Quickly, we raced back to the bleachers. Petrova was stretched out flat on her stomach again, waving at the chickens to keep them calm. Clementine was sitting back on her hind legs. They both looked very still-worried.

"So, what are we going to do with these?" Stella asked, holding up her oil can.

"When I used extra oil on Clara's unicycle, it went too slippy and she almost crashed," I said. "So if we rub a bunch on the chicken's feathers, they'll be oily enough to unstick from under the bleachers."

Stella looked like she wasn't sure. But then she shrugged. We didn't have any better ideas.

I leaned down and called to the chickens in my softest voice. One by one, they waddled over to me, as close as they could (Oona leading the way, of course). I poured oil all over my hands until they were super slidey. Then I rubbed those chickens' feathers so that they were slick-slick-slick, too.

Slowly, I wiggled Oona through the slats of the bleachers. She cooed a little, but mostly she was very brave.

Sliiiip! Out she popped!

"Yay!" She was free. I hugged her slippery-ish little body, and she gave me a thank-you flap of her wing.

She clucked at Loona and Maude so they'd know she was fine. Clementine made a little happiness trumpet.

Next came Loona and Maude. Maude was a tiny bit shaky when it was her turn. But sure enough, we got

those chickens nice and slippy, and out they came! When they were all safe and sound, there was lots of cheery clucking and trumpeting (and also laughing and relief-sighing from the actual human people).

"We did it!" I said to Stella. We did a giant squish-hug for saving the day.

I was just the proudest. Yes, I made an *eensy* mistake when I was bathing the chickens. *But* then I solved the problem!

"That was some good *eureka!* thinking, Louise!" Stella said. She smiled at me.

"I couldn't have done it without you," I told her.

FACT: Some of the best eureka! ideas start with BFF talks!

"Chuck Cluck will be back soon," I said.

We looked at the three chickens. They were still very drippy with oil. Stella said, "We need to clean you guys off for real before he gets here!"

Clementine pointed with her trunk. She led the three of us back to the bathing pen. Petrova and Stella filled one of the bigger tubs with water. I lifted the chickens into the bath.

And then! Clementine used her trunk *as if it was an actual hose!*

She sucked up the water in her trunk and sprayed it all over the chickens until they were squeaky-clean again. Then she sprayed me! Now I was all wet, but at least I wasn't muddy anymore. I laughed and laughed.

Asking my friends for help was probably my best *eureka!* idea yet!

"Louise! There you are!"

It was Chuck Cluck, back from Funky Town. And right behind him were Mama and Daddy.

13

HAPPY-HAPPY-HAPPY

"Louise! You're soaking wet!" Mama's eyebrows went way-high-up on her forehead. "Chuck told us he had to leave the chickens with you while he dealt with an emergency. Did everything go okay?"

"Everything went *perfect*!" Stella said quickly. "Lou just wanted to give the chickens a bath after their snack time."

Stella reached over and gave my hand a best-friend squeeze. I squeezed her hand right back.

FACT: Friendship hand squeezes are the coziest!

I could tell Mama wasn't sure she was getting the whole story. But she didn't ask any more questions.

"A bath! That's great!" Chuck Cluck said. "That'll save me a bunch of time tonight."

"Well, Lou," Daddy said, "we had our doubts when you talked to us this morning. But I guess this is proof—you're getting more responsible every day."

"Holy trapeze!" I shouted.

I did it! I showed Mama and Daddy real live proof of being grown-up-ish!

Yes, I spilled the spaghetti.

Yes, I got water in Clementine's ear.

Yes, I overoiled Clara Bear's unicycle.

And, yes, I accidentally a-little-bit lost the juggling chickens.

But then, with help from my friends, I found them again!

Now the chickens were squeaky-clean and Chuck Cluck was extra happy.

Everything was totally and completely almost perfect.

But there was one more thing I had to do to make this the extremely best day ever.

"I have something to show you," I told Chuck Cluck.

I poured some of the bubble-gum soap into one of the smaller tubs. Then I nodded at Oona, Loona, and Maude. They bobbed their heads at me for a minute, thinking in a chicken way. Slowly, they made their little chickeny *aha* faces. Oona waved one wing at her sisters so they'd follow her lead.

They chicken-walked over to the tub. One by one,

they dipped their beaks into the soapy water. Then they each bobbed their heads back up and squawked.

Cluck! Oona blew a perfect, shimmery soap bubble.

Cluck! Loona blew an even bigger bubble! It floated up to Clementine's forehead and *pop-pop-pop*ped.

Cluuuuck! Eensiest little Maude blew the very biggest bubble of all times! It landed on Chuck's nose.

Everyone burst out laughing. I was *happy-happy-happy!*

"It's a new trick!" I said. "We learned it today. What do you think?"

Chuck chuckled. "I think it's one hundred percent perfect," he said with a wink.

FACT: One hundred percent is the most percent you can have! It's my favorite of all the percents.

Mama, Daddy, and Chuck made a *glance* over my head. That meant they were thinking serious thoughts.

"I know Louise is doing her special tightwire routine tomorrow," Chuck said. "But do you think you could spare her for the chickens' act, too? Since she taught them to blow bubbles, she should be the one performing with them."

My eyes went wider than Tolstoy's hula hoops. "Are you for serious?" I asked.

"I for-seriously am," Chuck said.

Mama and Daddy looked at each other again. They both had thinking faces on. But they were smiling, too.

"That sounds like a great idea," Mama said.

"*Perfectamundo!*" I shouted.

I was still only seven years old. I had a long way to go before I'd be a real live grown-up who never, ever made mistakes.

But in the meantime, being just normal responsible Louise was a-okay. *Especially* when there were bubble-blowing juggling chickens around!

About the Author

MICOL OSTOW has never seen a juggling chicken in her entire lifelong time—yet. But she does have a French bulldog, who, sadly, does not know any circus tricks (though she is excellent at siesta-ing). Micol lives and works in Brooklyn, New York, where she reads books, drinks coffee, and usually tries her hardest to be a real live grown-up. (Sometimes it even works!) She is the author of numerous books for young adults and children, but Louise Trapeze is her first chapter book series. You can visit her at micolostow.com.

About the Illustrator

BRIGETTE BARRAGER is an artist, illustrator, designer, and writer of children's books. She recently illustrated the *New York Times* bestseller *Uni the Unicorn* by Amy Krouse Rosenthal. She resides in Los Angeles with her handsome husband, cute doggy, and terrible cat. Visit Brigette at brigetteb.com.

New friends. New adventures.
Find a new series . . . just for you!

FOR THE SPORTS FAN

FOR THE ADVENTURER

FOR THE SUPERSTAR

FOR THE DREAMER

FOR THE ANIMAL LOVER

FOR THE EXPLORER

RandomHouseKids.com